THE TEMPLE CURTAIN

Ruth Moblard DeYoung

Illustrated by Dan Drewes

WestBow Press books may be ordered through booksellers or by contacting:

WestBow Press
A Division of Thomas Nelson & Zondervan
1663 Liberty Drive
Bloomington, IN 47403
www.westbowpress.com
1 (866) 928-1240

Because of the dynamic nature of the Internet, any web addresses or links contained in this book may have changed since publication and may no longer be valid. The views expressed in this work are solely those of the author and do not necessarily reflect the views of the publisher, and the publisher hereby disclaims any responsibility for them.

ISBN: 978-1-4908-2741-4 (sc)
ISBN: 978-1-4908-2742-1 (e)

Library of Congress Control Number: 2014903652

Printed in the United States of America.

WestBow Press rev. date: 4/7/2014

WESTBOW
PRESS
A DIVISION OF THOMAS NELSON
& ZONDERVAN

CHAPTER 1 – THE HATED CRUTCHES

Shouts and laughter filled the air as the boys ran and played together. All except Nathan. He sat alone on the ground. Two battered wooden crutches lay next to him, thrown in the dirt.

"Stupid crutches!" he muttered, scooping up handfuls of dirt and pebbles and throwing them at his crutches. His scowl deepened as he stared at his weak, shriveled legs. "Useless legs! Can't run—or even walk!"

"Time for lessons," the rabbi announced. The other boys stopped playing, but Nathan continued to sit, staring at his crutches and tossing dirt on them.

"Come on, Nathan," called Benjamin, running over to him. "We need to go!" Nathan looked up and saw his cousin's strong, muscular legs. Tossing one last handful of dirt, he sighed deeply and slowly reached out to grab his crutches and shake off the dirt. Using hands and arms made strong by years of dragging lifeless legs, he pushed himself up and started toward the synagogue school with Ben.

Ben slowed down to walk with Nathan. "What's wrong? You're not usually so sad . . . and angry."

"I've been thinking about our future. We'll be turning thirteen soon. I'm part of Aaron's family and the tribe of Levi. I should be a priest when I grow up. And that's what I want!" Nathan frowned at his legs. "But I can't be a priest with my legs. I'll probably end up as a beggar."

"Nathan, you're the smartest boy at school. I don't know how you memorize all that stuff so easily. You could be a great scholar, studying the scriptures."

"But I want to be a priest like my father! I want to burn incense, sacrifice animals, and work for God in His temple. I'm not allowed to do that with crippled legs, and I couldn't do it with crutches anyway."

"Hey! I have an idea," Ben said, as they entered the classroom where the other students sat ready for instruction. "Rabbi's waiting. I'll tell you after school."

The boys sat cross-legged on floor mats as the rabbi led them in reciting the Torah, the books of the law. He asked questions which they answered from memory. Nathan tried to imagine what Ben's idea was. He usually had good ones.

"Nathan, please answer the question. Nathan?"

"Oh, I'm sorry Rabbi. I . . . I wasn't listening." The other boys looked at him in surprise.

When school was over at last, Ben and Nathan left together. "Okay, Ben, let's hear your idea."

"You've heard about that man Jesus who's going around teaching and healing people, right?"

"I've heard talk of him."

"That's my idea."

"What is?"

"We should take you to Jesus."

"To heal my legs?"

"I've heard he heals lots of people who are sick, blind, or crippled. Why not you?"

Nathan felt a small glimmer of hope. "Do you really think Jesus can heal my legs? And isn't he way up in Galilee?"

"I don't know if he can, but why not try? I heard he's in Judea now."

"I can't go far on crutches. I've never even been outside of Jerusalem."

"Maybe we can borrow a donkey."

"Yes, I could ride to find Jesus! I'll ask my father what he thinks, Ben. You ask yours." Nathan smiled and his eyes lit up. "This is a great idea!"

That night after supper, Nathan said, "Father, you've heard about a man named Jesus? I've heard that he heals people. Maybe he could heal my legs."

"I've heard that many go to him hoping to be healed. Because he's so popular, some of the priests are worried about what he may do."

"What do you mean?"

"The priests are afraid the people may try to make him a king. That would cause trouble with our Roman rulers."

"I just want to find him and ask him to make my legs strong. Please Father?"

"The things you hear about his power to heal may not be true, Nathan. I'd hate to have you get your hopes up and be disappointed. And how would you find him? How would you get to him on crutches?"

"Ben and I have a plan. We'll borrow a donkey to carry me. News of Jesus travels fast. I'm sure we can find him by asking people."

Eli frowned. "I wonder if Jesus can really do all the miracles people are talking about."

"Don't you think it's worth asking him, Father? Just imagine if I could walk and run. I could help more at home. If I had strong legs, I'd be able to be a priest in God's temple when I grow up!"

"I can see that you really want to try, so I'll talk to your Uncle Simon. I'd like to take you myself, but it's my time of service in the temple."

A few days later, Nathan rode on a borrowed donkey. His crutches, tied on behind him, knocked together as the donkey walked on the uneven terrain. They headed out of Jerusalem and into the Judean countryside. Uncle Simon led the donkey and Ben walked next to it. Nathan sat on the donkey, holding tightly to the donkey's mane with his hands, since his legs were powerless to grip the donkey's back. They looked out over green and brown rolling hills with occasional herds of sheep. Masses of dark green trees decorated distant ridges. When the donkey tried to stop and eat grass, Nathan urged him on.

"Look!" yelled Ben, pointing. "Crowds! Maybe that's where Jesus is."

Uncle Simon asked some men, "Do you know where we can find Jesus?"

A man pointed. "See where all those people are heading? That's where the teacher is."

Nathan saw people streaming from every direction, all heading toward a distant spot where a large crowd had already gathered. To Nathan, the donkey seemed to take forever as it stumbled down the rocky slope. When they reached the edge of the crowd, Nathan slid off the donkey and untied his crutches while Uncle Simon secured the donkey's rope to a small tree. People jostled and thronged from every side—mothers carrying fussy babies, fathers with little children on their shoulders, and old people bent over in pain.

"Please," Nathan said to a man in front of him. "I need to get through here to see Jesus. I want to walk."

"Nathan, throw down your crutches and walk."

"We need to see him too. See my daughter? She's blind." Nathan looked at a little bare-footed girl riding on her father's hips and clutching his arm. The man was tall and strong, with dark hair and a kind face. He gave his daughter a gentle hug and a tickle that made her giggle. "Martha, soon we'll see Jesus and you'll be able to see."

After what seemed like hours, Nathan said, "Uncle Simon, do you think it will ever be my turn to see Jesus? The sun's hot this afternoon and I'm thirsty. I wish we hadn't left our water skins on the donkey."

"Do you want me to run back for them?" offered Ben.

"Stay, Ben," said his father. "You don't want to miss seeing what happens when Nathan gets to see Jesus."

At last they were in front of Jesus. He wore a loose saffron-colored robe, the color typically worn by teachers. It accentuated his dark brown hair and beard and deeply tanned skin. Jesus smiled and said, "Nathan, come here."

He knows my name, thought Nathan.

"Why did you come here from Jerusalem to find me, Nathan?" asked Jesus.

"Please, Jesus, I want strong legs to walk and run. When I grow up, I want to be able to serve God in the temple like my father does."

"Do you believe that I can heal you?"

"I . . . I hope you can heal me. I really want to believe that you can. I'm trying hard to believe, but . . . my legs have always been like this."

"Nathan, throw down your crutches and walk." Nathan gripped his crutches more tightly. He looked down at his legs. They were still the same useless legs he'd always had. He was sure that if he dropped his hated crutches and tried to walk, he would fall flat on his face in front of all the people gathered around Jesus. He was confused because he thought Jesus would touch his legs to make them strong like those of other boys. The crowds around Jesus murmured and pushed inward, impatient for their turns to see Jesus.

Nathan looked up at Jesus, who smiled again and nodded toward Nathan's crutches. Nathan took a deep breath, bit his lip, and let the crutches fall from his hands. Keeping his eyes on Jesus, he took one small, tentative step . . . then another. He could move his legs for the first time in his life. He was walking! Nathan smiled at Jesus. Then he turned away from Jesus, pushed through the crowd, and tried running—first slowly, then faster—up and down and across the nearby hillside doing what he had previously done only in his most wonderful dreams. He twirled around and jumped as high as he could. Ben joined him and they raced together, finally falling down laughing.

"You can run as fast as I can," said Ben breathlessly. He hugged Nathan, and together they lay back to rest. Uncle Simon came up to them leading the donkey.

"Nathan, what a gift Jesus has given you! Let's start for home so we can share the news with your family."

"But Uncle Simon, I didn't say thank you to Jesus. I have to go back and thank him!"

"Look at the crowds, Nathan. Jesus is busy healing others who need him. You'll have to thank him another day."

On the way home, Nathan and Ben walked together in front of Uncle Simon and the donkey. When they were almost to Nathan's house, he ran ahead shouting, "Father, Mother, Rachel, Josiah, come out right away and see what Jesus did for me!"

Running up to Nathan, his father hugged him, tears in his eyes. "It's a miracle, a miracle by the power of Almighty God!"

With tears of joy streaming down her face, Nathan's mother embraced him, holding him close. Then Nathan grabbed his four-year-old brother Josiah and lifted him up, spinning him around in the air. Josiah laughed and squealed in delight.

Nathan hugged his ten-year-old sister Rachel who was, at first, speechless. Then, "Oh, Nathan, I'm so glad that Jesus made you well!"

Three children, joining hands, walked, jumped up and down, skipped, and ran in a circle laughing. Celebrating!

CHAPTER 2 – CELEBRATION AND ALARMING NEWS

Rachel and Nathan ran to the door of their home and looked out.

"There he is!" shouted Nathan.

They bolted out the door and raced down the dirt road to meet their father who was returning from the temple. Eli was thrilled to see Nathan running with legs only recently healed by Jesus.

"Father! Father!" exclaimed Rachel and Nathan. "You're home! We thought you'd never get here." Eli laughed as he hugged his children. He was happy to see how excited they were about the coming celebration.

"Our aunt, uncle, and cousins have been here for hours," said Nathan.

"And our grandparents just arrived," said Rachel.

"Well, now we're all here for our Passover meal," Eli said, "but you know we can't start until after the sun sets."

As they began walking back to the house, Eli linked arms with one child on each side and nodded toward the west where the sun glowed red and gold near the horizon. "Look, the sun is going down. Soon we can start our Passover meal and celebration."

As they walked back together, Nathan said, "Father, you were really busy at the temple today, right?"

"Right indeed," answered Eli. "Thousands of Jews from all over come to Jerusalem for the seven day celebration of Passover. Such crowds in the temple today!" Eli was pleased that Nathan was so interested in his work. Nathan would be a good priest some day. As they entered their home, Eli greeted his guests and swept Josiah into his arms for a big hug.

Eli smiled at Rachel and said, "Please help your mother now." As she skipped away, Eli delighted in how the recently lit oil lamps reflected off Rachel's beautiful black hair.

Turning toward Nathan, he asked, "Does Josiah know the questions to ask?"

"Yes, Father, I've been helping him learn them all week."

Soon Mother came in and lit the Passover candles. "Nathan, please tell Josiah and your cousins Ben and Abigail that it's time to wash and come for our meal."

Mother and Rachel laid out the food. With the family and their guests seated around a low table, Eli led in prayer: "Blessed are You, O Lord our God, King of the Universe, the creator who brings forth bread from the earth."

All joined in singing a Passover psalm: "From the rising of the sun to its setting the name of the Lord is to be praised!" For their special meal, they would eat matzah, cooked apples mixed with ground nuts, bitter herbs dipped in salt water, and roasted lamb. This perfect lamb had been taken to the temple early in the day for the Passover sacrifice. Then the lamb had been grilled on skewers made of pomegranate wood.

"Mmm," said Nathan. "The lamb smells delicious."

"My favorite is the apples and nuts," said Rachel.

"Why is this night different from all other nights?" asked Josiah.

Eli looked at his wife. "Thank you for cooking a splendid Passover meal, Sarah."

Sarah smiled at Rachel. "I had some excellent help."

Josiah was eager to do his part as the youngest child in the family. "Why is this night different from all other nights?"

"Tonight is special because we are celebrating the Passover to honor God and remember how he helped our ancestors, the Israelites, long ago. Who knows what 'ancestors' means?"

Father let Abigail answer. "It means our great, great, great, great, great grandfathers and grandmothers."

"Yes, Abigail, it was many, many 'greats' ago—hundreds of years. Our ancestors were slaves and worked very hard for a pharaoh who ruled Egypt. We're celebrating the night that God helped them get away. This pharaoh would not let God's people go. If they left, he wouldn't have all those slaves to work for him! Just imagine the huge crowd of people that God helped to leave Egypt. There were 600,000 men plus all their wives and children.

"Father," said Nathan, "may I tell the next part, please?"

"All right, Nathan."

"Pharaoh kept refusing to let the Israelites leave Egypt, so God punished the Egyptians to free our people. On the night of the first Passover, God was going to send an angel to kill every first born person and animal in Egypt. In our family, I'm the oldest. I might have died."

"That would have been awful," whispered Rachel.

"But God kept our ancestors safe," Nathan continued. "God told Moses, their leader, that each family should roast a lamb for supper and put its blood on the sides and tops of their doors. God's angel passed over the houses where people had obeyed God. Of course, we would have marked our door and the angel would have passed over our house. That's why we call our celebration tonight 'The Passover.'"

Eli nodded to Josiah who asked, "Why are we eating only . . ."

Noticing Josiah's hesitation, Nathan whispered "unleavened" in his brother's ear.

"Why are we eating only unleavened bread tonight?" Josiah looked at his father and Eli smiled approvingly.

Eli continued, "Our people were getting ready to run away from Egypt. They didn't have time to put yeast into the bread and let it rise that night, so they ate unleavened bread. Then they packed the extra dough and took it along into the desert where they baked it on rocks made hot by the sun. We remember this by eating flat bread called matzah. We call it unleavened because there is no yeast in it to make it bigger and softer."

"I like it," said Josiah. "It crunches. Usually we eat all kinds of herbs. Why are we only eating bitter herbs tonight?"

"The bitter herbs remind us of how terrible it was to be slaves in Egypt," Father answered.

"Why must we dip the herbs two times in salt water tonight?" asked Josiah.

"We dip our herbs in salt water to remember the tears of our ancestors in Egypt where the pharaoh treated them very cruelly. The fruit and nut mixture reminds us of the clay that our ancestors were forced to make and form into bricks for the pharaoh in Egypt."

"Why are we lying down to eat?" Josiah asked.

"We're lying down, leaning on pillows, because God set us free. On the night of the first Passover, our ancestors ate with their sandals on, standing up ready to leave. But we can relax."

After the meal and ceremony were concluded with songs of praise, the younger children played and the women cleaned up. Nathan and Ben stayed at the table with their fathers and grandfathers.

"I heard a rumor today," said Eli, frowning, "that some high ranking priests are secretly plotting to have Jesus arrested tonight. I fear that Jesus may be crucified tomorrow."

Nathan's eyes widened. He felt as if someone had kicked him in the stomach. "Arrested tonight? Killed? But why? He's kind and good!" Tears began to form in Nathan's eyes. "He healed me and so many other people and . . . oh no! I was so happy and excited when Jesus healed me that I went running and jumping and I never went back to thank him. If they kill him, I'll never be able to thank him."

Eli looked at his son, his eyes filled with concern as he saw Nathan's distress. "Oh Nathan, I know you love Jesus. His miracle changed your life and ours. But some priests say that Jesus is stirring up trouble with his teachings. Since the Romans rule our country, these priests think we need to be cautious and try to avoid trouble with the Roman rulers."

"Avoid trouble by killing Jesus? No!" Nathan yelled. He put his head down, hands covering his face, wiping away tears.

After a few minutes, Nathan looked up. "Maybe Ben and I could go into Jerusalem tomorrow. There's no school because of Passover. Please, Father!" He and Ben exchanged glances. "Maybe Jesus will do a miracle to keep people from hurting him. Oh, I hope so. May we go, please?" Nathan looked at his father, pleading.

"That's not a good idea, Nathan. Searching for Jesus in Jerusalem might mean going to the place of crucifixion outside the city. That's not something for you boys to see."

"But, Father, Ben and I are nearly thirteen. That means we're almost men now. And I really, really need to see Jesus. If he is going to be killed, it's my last chance to thank him."

"Well, all right, Nathan, but in the morning you must first help your mother. Feed and milk the goats, sweep the roof, and see what other chores she has for you. Jerusalem is very crowded, so be careful. I want to know what happens, but I'll be busy in the temple. You can tell me everything when I get home."

"Thank you, Father. We'll be careful."

Ben looked at his father, who nodded. "You may go with Nathan, but be sure to stay together."

CHAPTER 3 – A LIFE CHANGING LOTTERY

Early the next morning, Friday, Eli got ready to go to the temple. The sun was already getting hot. He waved to Nathan who was on the roof sweeping.

"Daddy, Daddy!" Josiah reached both arms up toward his father and Eli swung him off his feet and into his arms.

"I'm sorry, Josiah, I can't play with you now. I'm going to God's house. Maybe Rachel will play with you today." Josiah, brown eyes smiling playfully, tugged at Eli's neatly trimmed black beard. Kissing him on the forehead, Eli put down his son and hugged Rachel and Sarah. He turned and started down the dirt road.

As he walked briskly toward the temple, Eli thought about what would likely take place today—Jesus' death. He remembered the brief conversation he'd had with Sarah last night. Their bed had been rolled out on the floor ready for sleep. As they sat together, he had told her about the rumor and asked, "What do you think about a plot to get rid of Jesus?" Sarah had not answered. She had seemed deep in thought and her smooth brow was furrowed. He had pressed her. "Sarah, do you think it's right?"

She had turned slowly to face him. "Nathan would not be able to walk if it hadn't been for Jesus. Of course the priests shouldn't be plotting to have him killed."

Arriving at the temple, Eli purified himself in a special pool. He put on his priestly clothes beginning with knee-length linen pants. Then he slipped his white linen tunic over his head. It covered him from his neck down to his ankles and wrists. He wrapped his long, colorfully embroidered belt around his waist several times and tied it. Finally, he placed his white turban on his head. Walking barefoot, as required, he quickly went into the temple's inner courtyard.

There were fewer worshippers than usual. Outside in the city, great mobs of people crowded the streets. Eli could hear the distant shouts and commotion and would have liked to be out among them. Death by crucifixion was not something he ordinarily wanted to see, but this was Jesus, the man who had given Nathan strong legs, and a joy and confidence that he'd never known before. Maybe Jesus would save himself as Nathan hoped.

In the inner courtyard, Eli met the other priests. Some had slept at the temple in order to begin preparing for the day's worship before dawn. The priests gathered in the Chamber of Hewn Stone. Standing in a large circle, they held four lotteries to assign a long list of jobs and rituals related to the temple sacrifices. After some tasks were completed, all the priests serving at the temple that day met in the chamber to pray and recite the Ten Commandments.

The third lottery was special. It was held to choose someone to burn incense in the Holy Place. Each priest could do this only once in his entire life. Eli had never performed the incense sacrifice, so he stood in the circle of priests. When Eli was chosen, his heart soared. This was an honor and privilege that all the priests loved and desired. He had hoped for this moment ever since he began his priestly duties.

Each priest hoped that he would be chosen to burn incense in the Holy Place.

Chapter 4 – Darkness and Disobedience

While Eli was at the temple, Nathan and Ben were eating lunch at home with Sarah, Rachel and Josiah. They were enjoying fresh figs, goat cheese and flat, pancake-like loaves of warm barley bread. Suddenly, everything became dark.

"Hey, what's happening?" Ben yelled. "I can't see a thing."

"I know you're right there next to me, Ben, but I can't see you at all." said Nathan.

"Mommy!" called Josiah. "Where are you?"

"Right here, Josiah." Sarah reached over until her hand touched him. She picked him up and Josiah clung tightly to her. As they all fumbled their way toward the door, they kept bumping into each other in the thick darkness. There was not a glimmer of light anywhere. Finally, they stumbled outside. The sky was completely dark, as if someone had flung a heavy, black curtain over everything.

They stood there in silence. Finally, Nathan whispered, "It looks like the middle of the night, but with no moon or stars. How can this be?"

"I can't believe how dark it is," whispered Ben.

"What made it so dark?" asked Rachel, a quiver in her voice betraying her fear. Nathan put an arm around his sister. As they stood in their garden, small spots of light began to glow in the homes of neighbors.

"Nathan, come help me find and light our oil lamps. Ben, will you please stay out here with Josiah and Rachel?"

When two lamps were lit, Ben came in with Josiah and Rachel. Nathan whispered to Ben, "Now that people are lighting lamps, do you think we could find our way into the city? I really need to thank Jesus. We can see if what my father said last night is true, and maybe find out why it's so dark."

"Let's try," whispered Ben. "We know the way."

"Nathan," said Sarah sternly, "your father did not know it would be completely dark in the middle of the day. You can't go now."

"Please, Mother? I may never get another chance to thank Jesus. We'll be careful!"

"Absolutely not, Nathan!"

"Well, may Ben and I sit out in this strange darkness for a little while?"

Sarah nodded and the boys went back outside. After a few minutes, Nathan whispered, "Let's go anyway, Ben."

"But your mother said we couldn't go."

"I know, but our fathers both said we could, right?"

"They didn't know about this darkness."

"I'm going anyway! Are you coming?"

Quietly the boys left the garden and headed toward the center of the city. They walked arm in arm ever so slowly along the dark road, taking small, careful steps. Out of the darkness a dog barked. Goats bleated. They were able to find their way by watching for the flickering light of occasional fires and the glow of oil lamps burning in homes near the road.

"Your mother will be worried," said Ben.

"I know, and my father will be angry—and disappointed. I know what I'm doing is wrong, but I have to find Jesus and thank him."

Half an hour later, they reached the city gates. On a hill just outside the city wall, the boys saw a fire barely illuminating clusters of people around three crosses.

"Do you think Jesus is on one of those crosses?" asked Ben as they walked slowly up the hill.

"I hope not." But as they came near the crosses, tears welled up in Nathan's eyes as he choked out the words, "Oh, no! It's Jesus on the middle cross." Around Jesus' cross, they could make out soldiers, priests, and some women weeping. The boys edged closer.

One of the priests yelled at Jesus, making fun of him and saying, "If you really are the Messiah like you've said, come down from the cross. Then we'll believe in you."

Nathan was bewildered. Jesus only did good things. He whispered to Ben, "I don't understand why that priest is mocking Jesus. He serves God in the temple like my father, but he and other priests want Jesus dead. Why? Father said that Jesus could only heal me by God's power."

The boys heard one criminal say to Jesus, "If you're the Messiah, save yourself and us!"

But the other criminal scolded, "Be quiet. This man hasn't done anything wrong like we have." Looking at Jesus he said, "Lord, remember me when you come into your kingdom."

Jesus looked kindly at the second criminal and said, "Today you'll be with me in paradise."

"What kingdom is that man talking about?" asked Ben.

Nathan whispered, "I don't know about a kingdom, but Jesus did things that only God can do, right? Like heal my legs. Maybe he's the promised Messiah."

"I've heard that his disciples think so, but now he's going to be dead soon, so how could he be?" Ben whispered back.

Nathan looked intently at Jesus hanging on the cross and saw how much he was suffering. Blood was dripping from his hands and feet where huge nails pierced them, holding him on the rough wood of the cross. His face was bloody because a crown of thorny branches was stuck into his head. Nathan tried to get close enough to thank him.

"Move back, boy," said a soldier, pushing him roughly.

"But . . . I need to thank Jesus. I'd never walked in my whole life until he healed me."

The soldier sneered, "Oh yeah? He saved other people, but look at him. He can't save himself."

Nathan pushed nearer to Jesus. When he was close enough, he looked up and tried to speak, but no sound came out. Jesus looked directly at Nathan. As Nathan looked back at Jesus, he felt that Jesus knew everything about him and knew that he had come to thank him. Nathan's eyes filled with tears for Jesus. *His pain must be unbearable! Why is he dying? Why don't people stop taunting him? Why, why, why doesn't Jesus, who healed me and so many others, save himself now?*

In spite of the horrors of the scene, the boys stayed, wanting to see what would happen. After a long time, Jesus cried out in a loud voice saying, "My God, my God, why have you forsaken me?"

Nathan grabbed Ben's arm and held it tensely. "How could God leave Jesus to suffer alone?" he gasped.

Jesus cried, "It is finished," and died. Immediately, the boys felt a powerful earthquake shake the ground they were standing on, causing them to lose their balance and tumble down. Everyone standing near the crosses fell. Loose stones and pebbles rolled about. Then the violent shaking stopped.

"The darkness is gone," whispered Nathan. "It disappeared as suddenly as it came."

The boys heard one soldier say quietly, "This man surely was the son of God."

The boys got up and ran as fast as they could toward home until they were out of breath. As they slowed to a walk, Nathan said, "I want to ask my father what all of this can mean."

"Your father will be angry."

"I know, but he'll want to hear all about what we saw today. When Jesus died, there was a violent earthquake and that strange darkness disappeared!"

CHAPTER 5 – A SHOCKING EVENT IN THE TEMPLE

Earlier at the temple, the complete darkness that descended on the city at noon had caused great confusion. With only the light of the fire burning on the courtyard altar to help them, the priests had to find and light torches so they could continue doing their work.

When the time came for the sacrifice of incense, Eli threw down a large brass vessel called a magrepha. Its deafening sound could be heard miles away and called the priests, Levites, and other worshippers to the temple's inner courtyard.

One priest entered the Holy Place to clean the menorah and replenish its oil. When he finished, he lay face down to worship, stood up, and left. Another priest carried a gold shovel of burning coals from the huge stone altar in the inner courtyard. He arranged the coals on the incense altar, prostrated himself in worship and exited the Holy Place.

Eli and the priest who would assist him climbed the twelve steps up to the Holy Place. With expectant joy, Eli entered the Holy Place with a gold vessel containing specially prepared incense. The Holy Place was dark, lit only by the burning olive oil on its large seven-branched gold menorah. The other priest placed incense in Eli's palms. Slowly and carefully, so as not to burn himself, Eli sprinkled the incense on the golden altar, focusing his thoughts on the worship of his creator. He felt close to God in this place and savored his sacred duty. The smoke from the incense rose straight up, and filled the Holy Place with a cloud of smoke and the sweet smell of incense. He and his assistant lay face down in prayer and worship.

Eli wondered; *does this strange darkness have something to do with the crucifixion of Jesus? After all, Jesus claimed to be God's son, making himself equal to God. And he healed Nathan. Could Jesus' claims be true? Could he be the promised Messiah? The older priests seem so sure that arresting Jesus was for the best. They claim things will be better now that the "so-called teacher" will be gone. But it makes no sense to kill a teacher and healer.*

They got up and the other priest left, but Eli lingered. He stood looking toward the Holy of Holies studying the thick, heavy curtain just behind the incense altar. *A forever barricade, a wall separating us from God*, he thought. *Each year on the Day of Atonement the High Priest goes beyond that curtain to enter into God's presence. Only the High Priest may go inside and only to offer sacrifices for the sins of all the people, including his own.*

Suddenly, Eli felt the earth begin to quake. As he looked at the thick curtain, a shiver of apprehension passed through him. He watched in awe and horror as the curtain slowly and deliberately began to separate, torn by an unseen power, beginning at the top.

The earthquake was shaking the very foundation of the temple, but Eli's eyes were transfixed on the curtain. He was terrified now. He wanted to scream, to run, but he stood still, every muscle of his body tensed, unable to move. The loud grating sound of tearing cloth filled the room. He watched the tall blue, purple, and crimson curtain become two pieces—their jagged edges revealing the interior of the Holy of Holies.

The earthquake suddenly ceased. Eli smiled. He knew he had seen something very important. He felt that things would be different from now on, though he wasn't sure why or how. He felt that the torn curtain must have something to do with his relationship to God, whom he served in this place. He was puzzled, yet he felt excitement and peace.

Eli hurried out into the courtyard and joined the other priests who were standing on the steps in front of the Holy Place for the worship service. He noticed that the sun was once again shining brightly. The Levite choir had begun to sing and play their trumpets, lyres, and harps, filling the courtyard with the music of worship. They sang words from Psalm 93, "The Lord reigneth, he is clothed with majesty . . ." Eli was eager to share his news of the temple curtain, but he would have to wait.

Eli couldn't keep his mind on the service. His thoughts wandered to his family. *How did they cope during three hours of unexpected darkness? Josiah and Rachel knew nothing about what was probably happening on the hillside. Surely Nathan and Ben hadn't gone there in the complete and unnatural darkness. Or had they? What if they left home before the darkness came?*

Eli thought about what he had witnessed in the Holy Place. If he hadn't seen it, he would never have believed it could happen in God's temple. *Maybe God himself had torn the curtain?* He could think of no other explanation. None! *But, why? The curtain had separated God from His people. If God had torn it—the logical answer—then God had given them a sign!* Eli felt overwhelmed and waited impatiently for his chance to tell the other priests.

When the final song had been sung and the priests had extended their hands and given the blessing, Eli rushed over to the High Priest. "You and the other priests must come into the Holy Place. Something of great significance has happened."

"Whatever can you mean?" Caiaphas' penetrating dark eyes looked directly at him from below the gold crown he wore across his forehead. Its inscription read, "Holiness to the Lord." "The significant thing, Eli, is that we are through with Jesus of Nazareth. King of the Jews—ha! He is dead. Of that we are certain."

"When the earthquake began, the curtain in front of the Holy of Holies was ripped in half." Eli paused. He looked at his fellow priests and added with emphasis, "From the top to the bottom! Come and see for yourselves." The group made its way in silence, their robes making a swishing sound as they hurried up the steps to the temple and entered the Holy Place.

With clenched fists, Caiaphas, struggling to keep his voice to a whisper, said, "Who has desecrated the Holy of Holies in this way?"

"But, don't you see?" said Eli "This could only be the work of God!"

Terrified, Eli watched the temple curtain tear from top to bottom.

Chapter 6 – A Midnight Visitor

That evening, Eli and his family talked about their astonishing day.

"Daddy, it was so dark it was scary!" said Josiah.

"We couldn't see anything," said Rachel. "Mother lit some lamps, but it was still darker than night outside. Josiah and I sang songs and I told him stories."

"I liked the one about a big giant and David the shepherd boy," said Josiah.

"I'm glad you children found something to do in the dark." Turning to Nathan, Eli said, "I'm very disappointed that you disobeyed your mother and went into Jerusalem. You know what God's law says about honoring your mother and father."

Nathan hung his head as his father spoke. Then, looking at his mother, he said, "I'm very sorry for disobeying you." He knew it wouldn't do any good to give excuses like "You said it was all right," so he said, "Father, I'm sorry. I knew I was doing wrong, but I wanted so much to thank Jesus."

"And did you thank him, Nathan?"

"Ben and I went to the hill of crucifixion. We saw Jesus on a cross and listened to everything he said. When he looked at me, I knew he understood how thankful I am for my legs, even though I was speechless. Right after Jesus said 'It is finished,' he died. At that moment, the earthquake began and the darkness disappeared. We heard a soldier say that Jesus was surely the son of God. Could he be right? What do you think, Father?"

"Something astounding happened today at the temple. I was chosen to enter the Holy Place to burn the incense. Afterwards, I stood there alone looking at the curtain that separates the Holy Place from the Holy of Holies.

"Just as the earth started to shake, the curtain began to tear all by itself from top to bottom. From what you told me, Nathan, it happened when Jesus died." Eli paused to ponder the connection between the earthquake, the curtain, and Jesus' death.

"Was it dark in the Holy Place, Father?" asked Rachel.

"Yes, Rachel, it's always dark, except for the menorah burning."

"Can I see the torn curtain?" asked Josiah.

"No, son. Only priests may enter the Holy Place, but I can tell you all about it. The curtain is very tall and thick—as tall as twelve men and as thick as my hand is wide! It has always separated the Holy Place in the temple from the place we call the Holy of Holies where God is present. Now the curtain is torn into two pieces. I could look into the Holy of Holies. It's empty now, but the Ark of the Covenant used to be there."

"Why was it torn?" asked Nathan. "What do you think it means?"

"I'm not sure, but maybe God tore the temple curtain to tell us that now we're no longer separated from him. Our sins separate us from God, and we're all prone to sin. You demonstrated that today, Nathan. That's why the priests offer sacrifices every day in the temple. The tearing of the curtain happened at the precise

Jesus is alive! Nathan felt happiness exploding inside his whole being.

18

moment when Jesus died. There must be a connection between Jesus' death and the temple curtain tearing like that."

A week later, confused and dejected, Eli sat beneath the fig tree in his tiny garden. It was midnight. His family slept, but sleep would not come to him. The other priests had sneered at his conclusions, saying that the torn curtain was the "unfortunate result of the earthquake." Sarah had listened attentively and sympathetically, and for that he was thankful, but she was hesitant to fully accept his conclusions. Nathan was convinced that Jesus was a kind healer, but he had seen him die. He, Eli, was the only one who saw the tearing of the curtain, the only witness.

"Father? What are you doing out here?" It was Nathan.

"Can't you sleep either, son? I was just thinking about what I saw in the temple and what you saw on the hill of crucifixion."

All was quiet except for a gentle breeze rustling the leaves of their fig tree. Just then, the moonlight revealed a silent figure walking toward them. His sandals made a soft, shuffling sound on the road.

"Who would be coming toward our home in the middle of the night?" Eli wondered aloud.

Nathan gasped, "It looks like Jesus. But that can't be. No, I'm sure of it now. It is Jesus!"

Jesus entered the garden and said to Eli, "Don't doubt yourself and your conclusions. For years you and other priests have obeyed God's law with rituals and sacrifices, but the blood of bulls, goats, and lambs cannot take away sin. It is my sacrifice on the cross that takes away sin. I offered myself as a sacrifice for sin once for all time—for the sins of people in the past, present and future."

Turning to Nathan, Jesus said, "You will not grow up to be a priest in the temple. There's no need now for animals to be sacrificed for the forgiveness of sins. As the Lamb of God, I've broken the sin barrier that separated God and his people. God now welcomes you into his presence."

"But, if I'm not to be a priest, then what should I do?" asked Nathan.

"God will show you what to do when the time comes, Nathan."

There were a thousand more questions that Eli and Nathan wanted to ask Jesus, but instead they each embraced him. When Nathan felt Jesus' hands and arms around him, strong and alive, he remembered how they looked when Jesus was hanging on the cross. At that time, he could not have imagined this moment. Nathan was crying, smiling and laughing all at the same time and he felt happiness exploding inside his whole being.

After Jesus left, Nathan said to his father, "I need to tell the rest of the family. Now! I just can't wait until morning!" Although it was past midnight, he ran into the house.

"Jesus is alive!" he shouted. "Father and I saw him. We talked with him. He's alive!"

CHAPTER 7 – THROWN OUT

"Preposterous!" Caiaphas spit out the word angrily. "You know our position on the torn temple curtain—it was caused by the earthquake. Nothing more! And the empty tomb? Rubbish! Jesus' disciples stole his body to make people believe that he rose from the dead."

"I know what I saw, Caiaphas," said Eli, taking a deep breath to control his own anger. "The curtain tore from top to bottom at the very moment of Jesus' death. I wasn't sure of its significance until last night when Jesus came to our home."

Caiaphas' face was livid. "How dare you, a priest of the Almighty God . . ."

"My son and I talked with him. We touched him. He was not a ghost! Flesh and blood. Jesus is alive! And I believe that he is the Messiah we've waited for so long."

Eli returned Caiaphas' gaze, his eyes taking in the other priests who stood nearby dumbfounded. "Jesus explained to us that by dying on the cross he became the once and for all time sacrifice for sins. There's no need for us to continue to sacrifice animals."

"Then you can no longer be a priest here in God's temple!" Caiaphas spun around and stalked away.

Eli walked slowly to the room where the priestly garments were kept. He felt sad, yet expectant of what the future might hold. Taking off each piece of his priestly garments and putting them away for the last time, he prayed, "Lord God, now more than ever, I want to serve you. Show me how."

As he walked home, Eli wondered, *how will I explain to Sarah what happened at the temple? How will we live now without the tithes from the temple?* Eli heard footsteps behind him. Jacob, one of the other priests, hurried to catch up. Breathlessly, he exclaimed, "Eli, I want to know more. Tell me again what Jesus said when you saw him last night. Tell me how our sins can be forgiven by Jesus' death."

"Gladly, Jacob. Walk with me and we'll talk." As they reached his home, Eli said, "Would you like join us for supper?"

"I must go home to my family now, but I want to talk again soon."

As Eli opened the door, his three children rushed over to greet him. Josiah ran to him. "Daddy, Daddy!" Eli picked him up and kissed him, then gave his daughter Rachel a hug.

"You're home early today." said Nathan.

"Yes, Nathan, and it has to do with our conversation with Jesus last night."

"I don't understand, Father."

"The priests—most of them—refuse to believe what I've seen and heard. You heard Jesus say that we don't need to sacrifice animals any more, but these priests have spent their lives sacrificing animals to God for the forgiveness of sins. They can't imagine not doing it. Eli sat down, sighed, and rested his head in his hands. "And I'm no longer a priest in the temple."

Nathan walked over and put a hand on his father's shoulder. "I thought you would always be a priest. After Jesus healed my legs, I thought I would be one too . . . until Jesus came last night. What happens now? Should I stop going to school?"

Eli stood up and began to walk around the room. "No, Nathan, continue your studies. As followers of Jesus our Messiah, we'll continue to obey God's laws and commandments. I'm sure there are others—like

Jesus' disciples—who have accepted him as the Messiah. We need to work with them to tell others. After all these years of waiting for our Messiah, he is here. And yet even the temple priests don't recognize him."

That evening, Sarah frowned when she heard Eli's news. "But, if you're not a priest, how will we live?"

Eli moved closer to Sarah, put his arms around her, and held her close. "God will provide, Sarah. And I'm so glad that you believe with me that Jesus is our promised Messiah."

"I'm glad about that too. But everything has changed so suddenly.

CHAPTER 8 – A PROMISE

Each day, the believers met together to praise God in the temple and shared meals in each other's homes. Those who had food shared with those who did not. Jesus met with them, teaching them many things about God and his kingdom. Forty days after Jesus rose from the dead, he led his followers up a nearby mountain.

At the top, he turned and looked at them. "I'm leaving to return to my father in heaven, but don't despair! I won't leave you floundering around, not knowing what to do. Wait here in Jerusalem. You'll receive God's Holy Spirit. After that, you'll be witnesses for me. You'll start here in Jerusalem, then on to Samaria, and on to the ends of the earth. I will be with you!"

Nathan and Eli watched as Jesus raised his hands to bless them and then floated up from the earth toward heaven. He disappeared from sight, but all eyes remained fixed on the spot where he had vanished into a bright cloud.

"I've never seen a cloud as bright as that one," whispered Nathan.

Two angels appeared. "Why do you keep looking up where Jesus disappeared? Jesus gave you a job to do. Sometime in the future, he'll return, but don't stand here waiting for him."

Ten days later, Nathan studied his father's face, knowing that if he were still a priest, he might be serving at the temple on this special day. "Father, today's the Feast of Weeks. Are we going to the temple?"

"Of course, Nathan. Today is a joyous celebration of God's goodness in providing us with the harvest of grains for our food. Just because we no longer participate in the animal sacrifices of the day doesn't mean we won't go to the temple to worship in thankfulness. We'll leave as soon as everyone's ready."

"I'm ready," said Josiah.

"Good, Josiah," said Eli. "Mother and Rachel will be ready soon."

"Can we stop and ask Ben and his family to come with us—like they used to?" asked Nathan.

Eli sighed. "We can ask them, but you know they don't yet believe that Jesus is our Messiah. My brother-in-law can be very stubborn."

The family stopped at Simon's home. "Will you and your family come with us to the temple to celebrate the Feast of Weeks?" asked Eli.

"I thought you were no longer welcome in the temple," said Simon, a hard look on his face.

"I'm no longer allowed to serve as a priest there, but they cannot keep me from worshipping God in the temple. Many of us who have accepted Jesus as our Messiah gather on Solomon's porch every day to praise God for our salvation."

Ben, who was standing behind his father, locked eyes with Nathan. Nathan could tell that Ben shared his longing to be friends again.

"We'll go by ourselves." Simon abruptly closed the door in Eli's face.

As they walked together toward the temple, Nathan said, "I miss Ben! He's not only my cousin. He was my best friend. I don't understand. He and Uncle Simon saw Jesus heal my legs. Why won't they believe? Why does believing in Jesus have to keep us apart?"

"I miss seeing Abigail," said Rachel.

"I'm sorry that our new faith in Jesus has divided our family," said Eli.

"Remember when we celebrated Passover together?" asked Nathan. "We didn't know then that Jesus is our Messiah."

"Yes, son, and now it's fifty days—seven weeks plus a day—since the Passover celebration ended with the wave offering of barley. Today the priests will perform the wave offering of the two loaves of leavened bread."

"And it's been ten days since Jesus left us. What a surprise to see him rise up and just disappear. I'm glad we were there with his other followers."

"He gave us a promise that day. Don't forget that." Eli reminded Nathan. "He told us to wait here in Jerusalem for his Holy Spirit. I wonder how long we'll have to wait."

"Not much longer, I hope," said Nathan, as they began climbing together up the steep hill to the temple. At the temple, they joined the crowds of worshippers who slowly walked up a broad staircase. At the top, they entered through a wide, double gate into a series of passageways that led them into the temple's outer courtyard. Nathan heard people who had come from many different countries for the celebration talking in languages that he didn't understand.

As Nathan looked up at the temple, the bright morning sun reflected off its white limestone and gold walls so brightly that Nathan shielded his eyes. The followers of Jesus—more than a hundred of them—were gathering for worship in the courtyard. Nathan's family joined them.

Suddenly they heard a loud whooshing sound like a strong wind blowing among them. Nathan looked around to see where the sound was coming from. All Jesus' followers seemed to have flames of fire resting on top of their heads. Nathan thought, *I don't feel anything, but I must have one on my head too.* Then the flames and the sounds of wind disappeared.

The thousands of Jewish worshippers were dwarfed by the immensity of the temple courtyard. When they heard the wind and saw the commotion, many rushed over to see what the excitement was about. An enormous crowd gathered.

A man from Arabia said, "Why, I hear these men praising God in my own language! How can that be?"

"They must be drunk with too much wine," scoffed another man.

"I doubt that," said another. "I come from the Jewish community in Rome, and I'm also hearing these uneducated Galileans praising God in my language."

Nathan watched and listened as Peter began to preach loudly and boldly to the crowd that milled about. "Men, listen! These men aren't drunk. It's too early in the morning!"

Nathan whispered to his father, "I heard that Peter was afraid to admit he was one of Jesus' followers when Jesus was arrested. He's so different now. He doesn't seem even a bit afraid."

You're right, Nathan. He's bold because he's filled with God's Spirit. Let's listen." The stirring and murmuring of the crowd quieted.

Peter went on, "What you see happening here today is Joel's prophecy fulfilled: 'In the last days, I will pour forth my Spirit on all people. You and your sons and daughters will prophesy. I will show wonders in heaven and signs on the earth.'"

In the vast temple courtyard, Peter addresses thousands of worshippers with the message "Jesus is our Messiah."

As Peter talked about the sun turning into darkness, Nathan remembered the unbelievable darkness that had blackened the sky when Jesus hung on the cross. He recalled the violent earthquake when Jesus died and the sign in the temple—the tearing of the curtain. Nathan thought about what Jesus had said that night in the garden, "God will show you what to do." He thought, *I wonder if God wants me to tell others about Jesus, the Messiah. Could I be bold and unafraid like Peter?*

Peter continued, "All you members of Israel: I want you to know that Jesus, whom you crucified, is our Messiah."

"We have crucified the Messiah! What should we do?"

"We deserve God's anger. How can we escape?"

Peter answered, "Declare your sorrow for your sins and turn to your Messiah, Jesus, who is alive! All of you who accept Jesus as your Messiah must be baptized in his name. Your sins will be forgiven and you will receive the gift of the Holy Spirit."

"Father," asked Nathan. "Will they believe? God's priests in the temple didn't."

"But now, Nathan, we have God's Spirit sent to us as Jesus promised. God's power is at work. Look at all who are repenting." They watched in amazement as thousands of Jewish pilgrims and many temple priests knelt in repentance.

The crowds streamed out of the temple courtyard, through the temple gates, and down the stairs to a place outside where dozens of ritual baths were located. Nathan and his family went along to watch.

"Father, look!" Nathan pointed to a big square bath with steps on four sides. Many people stood together on the steps waiting to be baptized. "It's Ben and his family!"

"Praise God!" exclaimed Eli.

They worked their way through the throngs of new believers and watched as Ben's family was baptized. After they came out of the water and up the steps, Eli said, "I'm so happy that God has brought you to faith!"

Sarah and Josiah watched Eli hug his sister and then Simon. Abigail and Rachel ran together, hugged and stood arm in arm. Ben and Nathan stood together, smiling. "Ben, I've missed you so much!" said Nathan.

CHAPTER 9 – FLIGHT FROM PERSECUTION

Nathan and Ben pressed their backs against the wall, hiding in its shadow as best they could. "They took Steven into the council chamber," whispered Nathan. "He's been in there a really long time."

"God protected Peter and John. Won't he protect Stephen too?" asked Ben.

"Shhh, they're coming out now. They're pushing and shoving Stephen out of the city."

"They look angry! I wonder what happened in there."

The boys followed at a distance, getting as close as they dared. They saw men beginning to pick up large stones. "They're going to stone him," whispered Ben, "and there's nothing we can do."

"Stephen doesn't look scared or angry," whispered Nathan. "He looks like he's praying." As stones began to fly through the air, Nathan grabbed Ben's arm. "Let's get out of here!" The boys snuck away from the vicious stoning and ran to Nathan's house.

When Eli heard what Nathan and Ben had witnessed, he said, "I fear for our family. The chief priests seem determined to get rid of all those who believe in Jesus. They know me, where I live, and where I stand. They may come after us. We must leave Jerusalem."

"But this is our home. Where will we go?" asked Nathan.

"We'll head north, Nathan. God will be our guide."

"What about our grandparents? They've accepted Jesus as the Messiah. They'll be in danger too," said Nathan.

"Of course we'll take them with us. I'll make arrangements."

"What about my family?" asked Ben.

"We should flee together. I'll walk back with you and talk with your father."

A few nights later, dark clouds scudded across the sky, hiding the sliver of a moon that had shone earlier that night. Josiah opened sleepy eyes to see his father gently shaking him. Nathan, Rachel, Sarah, and her parents were already up, hastily packing clothes and food.

"Why are we getting up now?" asked Josiah. "It's dark outside. It's night."

"We're leaving Jerusalem, Josiah. We're sneaking out in the dark so we can get away without being caught."

"Why?" asked Josiah sitting up.

"Because there are people who want to arrest all the followers of Jesus and put us in prison. We're going to travel to a safer place."

Josiah, fully awake now, put on his robe and sandals. "Can we take our goats with us?"

"Yes, Josiah," said his mother. "We'll bring them along for milk and cheese."

As the family left the only home the children had known, Nathan said, "Father, what about Ben and his family?"

"They'll bring my parents to our chosen meeting place. From there we'll go on together."

The family carried their supplies and led their two goats out of the yard and up the road. Hidden by darkness, they walked silently until they were well away from the homes of neighbors and friends. North of Jerusalem, they found their meeting place, a cave.

"This is going to be an adventure," said Ben, hugging Nathan. Rachel and Abigail embraced.

"Best be going now that you're here," said Uncle Simon. "We should get as far as possible tonight."

As they walked on, two other families of believers joined them. "Good," said Eli. "When we go on the road down to Jericho it will be good to be in a large group. There's danger from robbers in that desert area."

After hours of walking, Sarah said, "We've walked many miles. Shouldn't we find a place to get some rest?"

They found shelter behind a large outcropping of rocks at the top of a hill next to the road. Shielded from the road, they lay down, huddling together for warmth and security.

As the sky began to turn yellow and pink with the morning sun, Nathan woke up and tapped Ben on his shoulder. "Let's go take a look at the road now that it's light."

Remembering what Eli had said about robbers, the boys stayed hidden in the shadow of the rocky hill. Suddenly Nathan grabbed Ben's arm and pointed down the road. They looked at each other, eyes wide with terror and muscles tensed. A gang of four strong men with big clubs dangling from their waists was walking up the road. The boys held their breath as the group walked on the road below their hiding place.

As Nathan and Ben leaned closer to the rocks to better hide themselves, a small stone dislodged and tumbled down toward the road below them.

"Hey, someone's up there!" shouted one of the men.

"Ben, stay hidden," whispered Nathan.

Nathan walked down the hill to the road where the robbers stood. He walked slowly, dragging one foot behind him as if he were lame. That wasn't hard. He'd had years of practice. *But what should I say?* The robbers looked menacing, but Nathan prayed silently and tried to act braver than he felt. "I ran away from home and was hiding up there. I know you men are robbers. Can I join you and be a robber too?"

The men sneered at the idea. "We don't need a cripple like you to slow us down."

"Go back to your cave, kid," said another robber. The men turned and continued down the road, laughing loudly. Nathan stood watching, not daring to go back to the group until the robbers were out of sight. Then he turned and ran up to where Ben was hidden.

"Nathan, you were so brave. If they had found us . . . I hate to think what they might have done! What did you say to them?"

"I asked if I could join their band of robbers."

"You said that? What if they had said yes?"

"I knew they wouldn't want someone with a lame leg to slow them down."

"How'd you think so fast?"

"I prayed. I'm sure God helped me think of what to do and say."

The boys sneaked back to the group. Everyone was still asleep. Nathan and Ben found their fathers and woke them.

Nathan walked down the hill to where four menacing robbers stood.

28

"Father, Ben and I saw a group of robbers walking on the road below. We were hidden by the rocks, but a small rock fell off and rolled down to the road as they were walking past us."

"What? They didn't come after you?"

"No, and that's because of Nathan's quick thinking and bravery," said Ben. "He fooled them by pretending to be alone and dragging one leg as he walked. They went on their way laughing at him."

"Why would they do that?" asked Uncle Simon.

"Because he asked them if he could join their band of robbers," said Ben.

"You boys put us all in danger by sneaking out like that," said Eli. "But now that we know how real the threat is, we must prepare."

"Even though our group has over twenty people, we only have six men and you two older boys," said Uncle Simon. "And no weapons."

"We can pray for God to keep us safe," said Nathan. "He helped me think of a way to get rid of the robbers."

An hour later, the group of Jesus' followers had worshipped and prayed together, and decided on the safest way to walk—a man in front, one in back, and two on each side with the women and children in the center. Nathan and Ben were the look-outs for their trip to Jericho. They walked ahead of the group, searching for any signs of danger. Once, the boys stopped and pointed toward a nearby hill. Some bushes were moving.

"Oh! Maybe there are robbers hiding behind those bushes," whispered Rachel.

The group stopped, wondering what to do. "I hope not, but it's possible," said Eli.

Then two goats emerged from behind the bushes and they all laughed, relieved that the "robbers" were only goats. After arriving in Jericho, they praised God for their safe trip.

The next morning, the men talked about where to go. Ben and Nathan listened.

"We should go to a city with a lot of people," said Eli.

"And somewhere far away from Jerusalem," said Simon.

"Could we make it as far as Antioch in Syria?" asked Eli. "I've heard that there are many Jewish people living there."

"How far is it?" asked Nathan.

"It's a long trip," said Eli. "We should pray for God's help in our decision."

"Let's continue north, one day at a time," suggested one grandfather. Now that we've made it to Jericho, we can follow the road along the Jordon River. It will be flat and easier walking."

So the group fled north out of Palestine, through Phoenicia and into Syria. They continued north toward the large city of Antioch on the Orontes River.

CHAPTER 10 – A NEW HOME IN ANTIOCH

After walking for more than two weeks and over two hundred miles, the weary travelers arrived in Antioch, a large city bustling with people and activity. At its entrance was a tall statue.

"Look at that statue of a woman," said Ben. "She must be six times as tall as I am."

"Who do you think she is?" asked Abigail.

"I imagine that's an idol," said Nathan. "Many people here probably worship idols."

"I think they worship Roman and Greek gods and goddesses," said Eli.

As they walked on, Nathan said, "Antioch is a lot bigger than Jerusalem!"

"It's a pretty city. Look at that beautiful mountain," said Rachel.

"Where will we keep our goats?" asked Josiah.

"We'll find a new home for them and for us, Josiah," said Sarah.

"Let's ask for directions to the area where other Jewish people have settled," suggested Uncle Simon. "We can ask a shop keeper at the market."

"Can you tell us how to get to the Jewish settlement?" Eli asked a man selling vegetables.

"Certainly. The whole southeast part of the city is a Jewish community. Just go down that road for about a mile."

"Thank you," said Eli, as he led the group toward their goal.

"We're finally near the end of our long journey," said Sarah. "But where will we stay? We can't just ask strangers to take in our big group of people."

"Maybe we can split up and stay with different families until we can find our own places to stay," said Eli.

"I miss our home," said Josiah, kneeling down to put an arm around his favorite goat's neck.

Nathan rested his hand on his brother's shoulder. "We all do, Josiah. But God has guided us here. He'll help us make a new home."

Josiah nodded uncertainly. "I guess so."

The families found places to stay and, in time, homes of their own.

"Father, now that we're settled here, what do you think God wants us to do? Remember what Jesus told me that night in the garden? That I would never be a priest? He was right about that! So how do I know what God wants me to do now?"

Eli stroked his beard thoughtfully. "Think about what Jesus told us on the mountain. He said to tell others about him to the ends of the earth. The people in Antioch need to hear about Jesus. We can start in the nearest synagogue, and go to the rest of the synagogues on other Sabbaths."

"Good, let's do that!" said Nathan.

On the next Sabbath day, they went to a nearby synagogue where many Jews and Gentile converts worshipped. Eli introduced himself as a former priest from Jerusalem and asked if he and Nathan might speak to the congregation.

Nathan spoke first. "When I was born, both my legs were crippled. I had never walked in my life. I dragged myself around on crutches, hating them and my useless legs. Then last year a teacher named Jesus healed my legs. Look at me now!

"But Jewish leaders in Jerusalem had Jesus put to death. I went to the place of crucifixion to thank Jesus for the miracle he did for me. While Jesus was hanging on a cross, the sun stopped shining and everything became dark. We couldn't see our hands in front of our faces! But when Jesus died, the sun was suddenly shining again, and an earthquake shook the earth beneath our feet throwing us to the ground."

Eli took over the story. "On the day Jesus died, I was the priest chosen to burn incense in the Holy Place in God's temple. After I finished the incense sacrifice, an earthquake began to shake the temple. But listen, all you believers in the one true God; at that moment the thick curtain that separates the Holy Place from the Holy of Holies tore all by itself from the top to the bottom!"

The synagogue was quiet as the congregation listened intently. Eli continued, "I felt that this must be a sign from God, but I didn't understand until Jesus—alive and risen from the dead—came to see Nathan and me in our garden at night. He told us that his death on the cross was God's plan for the forgiveness of sins for us, and for those in the past and in the future. I declare to you that Jesus is the Messiah promised to us for so many years! Trust in Jesus for forgiveness, repent of your sins, and be baptized."

Murmuring rose up among those gathered in the synagogue. Some said, "Our Messiah at last!" or "I'd like to know more." Others scoffed. Finally, the leader of the synagogue said, "Let each man consider the message and decide if he and his family will believe in Jesus as the promised Messiah."

Eli invited those who wanted to be baptized to come back to their home that day, and so a house of worship began in their home.

CHAPTER 11 – CHAOS IN THE MARKET PLACE

As the family ate breakfast one morning, Rachel said, "I'd love to go into Antioch today to see some of the flowers that are blooming. Could we walk around the city and find a public garden?"

"Well, Nathan and Ben are thirteen now. Perhaps they would go with you and Abigail—as long as you all stay together. Would you take them, Nathan?" asked Eli.

Nathan looked at his sister and nodded. "Of course. Ben and I know our way around the city pretty well."

Rachel smiled. "I can't wait to tell Abigail!"

Later, as they reached the market area, Rachel pointed, "Look at those men throwing and catching lots of balls all at once. How do they that?"

"I'm sure juggling takes a lot of practice," said Ben. "And look over there. Dancing girls."

"Their costumes are pretty," said Abigail. "I like the music,"

They walked past merchants selling fruits, vegetables, meat, pottery, cloth, jewelry, and other goods. Rachel stopped to touch some cloth. "Oh! It's so soft. What is it?"

"This is called silk. Made from the silk cocoons spun by caterpillars," said the merchant. "Comes all the way from China."

"Really? Caterpillars make this? It's beautiful," said Rachel.

"Come smell the spices for sale over here." called Ben.

"I like the smell of the perfumes," said Abigail.

"Oh, they don't smell nearly as nice as real flowers," said Rachel.

The marketplace was crowded and noisy as customers haggled for the best prices. Just then there was a commotion as people crowded aside to let some men pulling cages pass by. Inside the cages were large, brown bears.

"Where are they taking all the bears?" Nathan asked a man standing near him in the crowd.

"They're on their way to the circus. The bears perform tricks at the Hippodrome. That's also where chariot races are held."

The four stood together, watching the procession of caged bears. Suddenly, one of the wagons lost a wheel. As the cage fell sideways, the cage's latch popped open.

Rachel was the first to notice that one of the bears was pushing the cage door open with its nose. She grabbed Nathan's arm. "Nathan, look! The bears are getting out!"

"Stand very still," said Nathan. "Let's pray they don't come this way." He put is arm around Rachel and Ben did the same to Abigail.

Soon others closer to the accident saw the loose bears, and mass panic and confusion broke out. As people scrambled to get away from the bears, piles of red pomegranates spilled from a fruit seller's booth and went bouncing and rolling all over the ground. As another booth was jostled, statues of goddesses tumbled down, clattering as some fell on top of others. To escape the bears, some people headed toward the fountain in the middle of the marketplace. They jumped into the water, and even climbed up onto the fountain to escape the bears.

One bear started munching on pomegranates while the other bear headed toward the fountain. Screams filled the air as the people in and on the fountain scrambled out and ran. Two soldiers who had been stationed in the marketplace marched toward the bears with spears raised, ready to kill the bears.

"Stop!" yelled a bear trainer as he ran toward the soldiers from the caravan of bear cages. He held a whip in one hand and some food in the other. "Don't kill the bears! They're trained and I can get them back into their cages. Please, just turn the cage upright and open its door."

The soldiers obliged, and the trainer coaxed the pomegranate eating bear with his whip and a piece of fish. Finally, the bear walked away from the fruit and back into its cage. The other bear had climbed right into the fountain and was enjoying the water. Enticed by the smell of the fish, the bear lumbered over to the edge, climbed out, and shook himself, sending water spraying in every direction. Then the bear walked back to the cage and the trainer opened the door, let him in, and fastened the latch. "Now we'll fix that wheel and be on our way."

Once the bears were back in the cages, things gradually returned to normal. Rachel and Abigail helped pick up the pomegranates while Nathan and Ben helped pick up the idols.

When the pomegranates had been collected and put back into their baskets, and the idols had been picked up and returned to their display, the owner of the fruit stand said, "Thank you for being so kind and helping me."

"Yes, thank you," said the owner of the idols. "You were the only ones who stopped to help us with this awful mess."

"Our Messiah, Jesus, taught us to love others. We worship the one true God who made us and everything in the world. If you'd like to learn more about him, come to Eli's home in the Jewish section."

As the four of them left the market place, Ben said, "You're so bold, Nathan. You're never afraid to speak about Jesus, even to a seller of idols."

They arrived at a large public garden and began to walk around. "The sun makes the fountain sparkle like stars," said Rachel. "And I love the sound of the water falling. But, oh, look at all the beautiful flowers—so many colors!"

After enjoying the flowers, they began walking toward home. As they passed a public bath house Ben said, "Why don't we take a look? I've always wanted to see what their bath houses look like inside."

"Well, they're impressive from the outside. I guess we could take a quick peek," said Nathan. "The baths seem to be very popular, and there are lots of them because of all the springs here in Antioch."

They climbed up the stairs and stepped inside. "Look at all the people bathing in those beautiful, decorated pools," said Rachel.

"It seems to be a place to meet with friends," said Nathan. "The water looks inviting, but we'd better go."

As they walked away from the bath house, they heard footsteps behind them. A group of six teen-aged boys was following them. They walked faster, but the group of boys caught up and confronted them. "Look here. Four Christians—little Christs. Why did you come into our bath house today?"

"We were just curious." said Nathan. "And isn't it a public bath house?"

"I suppose, but I've never seen any Jewish people go into one."

Panic and confusion filled the marketplace as people tried to get away from two escaped bears.

"Say, what did you call us before?" asked Nathan. "Christians? Why?"

"'Christos' is our Greek word for messiah. People here have started calling you 'Christians'—you people who are always talking about a messiah named Jesus."

"Well, I like that name," said Nathan. "Jesus is our Messiah and Savior, and if you want to find out how you can become Christians, come to our home in the Jewish part of Antioch. Ask directions to Eli's house."

The boys turned without responding, and hurried back toward the bath house. "Well," said Ben, "let's go home for lunch. Do you think those boys or the merchants will come to learn more about Jesus?"

"I don't know," said Nathan, "but . . . God's Holy Spirit can surprise us."

CHAPTER 12 – SAIL AWAY OR STAY?

It was a warm, sunny day with a brilliant blue sky. Nathan and Ben watched the ships in the Antioch harbor. The boys heard grunts and thuds as men loaded heavy barrels of dried fruit, grains, wine, and leather onto a sailing vessel in preparation for leaving the next day.

"It would be fun to sail away with Paul and Barnabas tomorrow. What an adventure that would be," said Ben. "I've never even been out in a small boat."

"They'll sail down the Orontes River first and then out into the sea on a bigger ship. They'll face unknown dangers, but . . . I've been thinking about asking Paul if I could go along to help them."

"Really? Wouldn't you miss your family and me? I'd miss you a lot! Would your father allow it?"

"I'm going to talk with Paul first to see what he says."

Later, Nathan had a chance to speak privately with Paul. "Paul, after Jesus rose from death, he came to our house. He said God would show me what I should do with my life, since I wouldn't be a priest. Maybe God wants me to go with you on your missionary trip."

"Nathan, I'm glad you're seeking God's will. John Mark is going along to help us. You've been a great help to Barnabas and me for the whole year that I've been preaching and teaching here in Antioch. I believe you can serve God better by staying here. Although you're only fifteen, God has already used you in Antioch."

"But how do I know what God wants? How did you know that God wanted you and Barnabas to go?"

"Through prayer, Nathan. Pray about it tonight and think about this: there are still hundreds of thousands of people here in Antioch who need to hear about Jesus. You're not afraid to speak boldly to others about the Messiah. You even spoke to an idol seller in the market place, and now he's a Christian!"

"All right, Paul, I'll pray and ask God to show me what to do."

The following morning, many Antioch Christians planned to gather at the harbor to say goodbye to Paul and Barnabas.

"Rachel, hurry up!" called Nathan. "We don't want to miss anything. Father, may Rachel and I go on down to the harbor now?"

Josiah jumped up and down excitedly. "Me too! Look, I'm ready."

"Go ahead," said Father. "Take Josiah along, but be sure to hold his hand when you're near the water. The harbor's deep. We'll meet you there."

At the harbor, they watched the sailors untying the ropes that secured the sails. The sails fluttered and flapped in the wind as the sailors pulled the ropes, hoisting up the huge sail for departure. Nathan saw Paul beckoning to him. "Rachel, hold Josiah's hand. I need to talk with Paul."

"Well, Nathan, has God made things clear?"

"Yes, Paul. I see that Antioch is where God wants me to be . . . teaching others about Jesus, our Messiah."

"Good. I'm glad you'll be telling others here in Antioch about Jesus while I'm gone. I'll pray for you, Nathan, and you pray for us." They joined the group at the wharf. It was a bustle of goodbyes, hymns, and prayers as the Christians said farewell to their missionaries.

As they walked home, Nathan said to his father, "God chose you to burn the incense on the day of Jesus' death. The tearing of the temple curtain has really changed our lives."

"The torn curtain was only a sign, Nathan. It is Jesus that has changed our lives."

In the Antioch harbor, a ship is readied. Paul and Barnabas are leaving to spread the message of Jesus to new places.